MERSEA MIC

By

Veronique Eckstein

Illustrated by **Tom Knight**

A Mersea Island Tales Book

This story is dedicated to Mersea Mick
and to all those dogs who serve their masters well.

A Mersea Island Tales Book
First published in Great Britain in 2012
www.merseaislandtales.co.uk
This book has been written and produced on England's most easterly inhabited island.
It has been printed on paper from sustainably managed forests.

Text copyright © 2012 Veronique Eckstein. Illustrations © 2012 Tom Knight
FIRST EDITION. All rights reserved
The moral right of the author and illustrator has been asserted.
Layout by Tom Knight. Printed by Healeys Print Group
ISBN 978-0-9563781-1-8
Cataloguing Data: A catalogue record for this book is available from the British Library.

FSC
www.fsc.org
MIX
Paper from
responsible sources
FSC® C006671

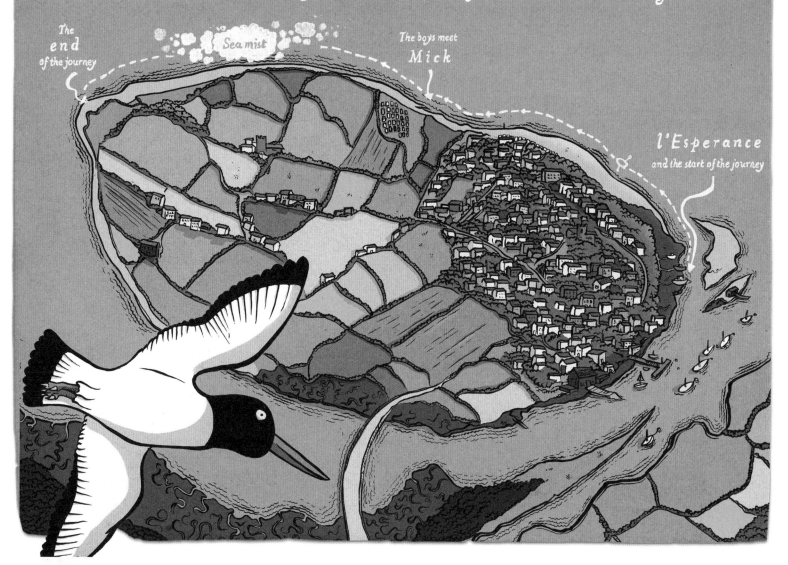

An inaccurate Map of
Mersea Island

showing the journey undertaken by Hamish and Angus

The
end
of the journey

Sea mist

The boys meet
Mick

l'Esperance
and the start of the journey

A story from
the East Coast of England

*Between the mouths of the rivers
Blackwater and Colne lies a marshy tract,
veined and freckled with water and islands.*

Sabine Baring-Gould

Mehalah

At least Hamish and Angus agreed on one thing!

Summer had really been summer.

The weather had been true.
The sun had shone.
The sky had been blue.

Best of all, the wind had blown southerly.

They had swum.

They had crabbed.

They had sailed.

They had laid in the sun
and dreamt.

They had played in the mud
until the last of the light
melted away on the marshes.

But today was different.

Today was the beginning of the end of the perfect summer.

School loomed and this was to be a day to remember, a day to hold onto when the routine of cold school mornings made the holidays a distant memory.

They had carefully planned how they were going to set off in their rowing boat, taking the early tide along the shore to arrive at the top of the island at noon where they would anchor and wait.

Wait exactly where the Battle of Britain Memorial Flight would pass overhead on its way towards the summer air show further along the coast at Clacton.

They began stowing their gear in the little locker at the front of the boat.

Just then, their father leant over the deck of the old houseboat and called down to them on the beach.

"Have a great day boys, don't forget your compass, radio and above all your lifejackets. Remember your safety at sea routine."

"Hurry up!"
yelled Hamish,
the elder of the boys,
annoyed that their father was
shouting instructions and delaying them.

"OK, OK", he called back, as he leapt into the boat, rapidly followed by his younger brother Angus. "We've got all that stuff, see you later this afternoon." And with that the boys began to pull on their oars, smoothly gliding through the clear salty water.

Half-way along the island they decided to stop for a rest. Tossing the anchor overboard, they jumped into the water and ran laughing up the beach.

Suddenly, from behind a twisted, gnarled tree stump leapt out the friendliest of fox terriers. For half an hour they raced and chased the dog up and down the beach, until finally, exhausted, they all flopped down in the sand to rest.

Sharing his ham sandwich with his newly found friend, Angus reached around the dog's neck and held onto the well-worn leather collar. The old brass dog-tag had the words "Mick, 1927" inscribed on it. "That's a bit short for an island telephone number", thought the boy, "mine's got at least six numbers."

"Come on, hurry up or we'll miss the tide, the current's changing already",
urged Hamish.

Just as Angus was running to join Hamish in the boat, Mick dropped
something at his feet. Not having time to inspect it, Angus put it in
his bag, hugged the dog and handed him the last of his lunch.

"Bye Mick, hope to see you again soon",
he whispered in the dog's ear.

But suddenly the boys realised, that in the short time they had been playing on the sunny beach, things had changed …

Now the sky was not blue, the sun was not shining and an eerie mist was rapidly descending on the river.

It was getting more and more difficult to see.

Although the boys felt they knew the island well, the sea-mist was swirling in so quickly and becoming so thick, that soon they could barely see the bow of their boat.

They began to panic. An icy thought crossed the older boy's mind. Where were their life-jackets? In their haste to catch the tide they must have left them hanging on the tree stump where, minutes earlier, they had been laughing and playing with Mick.

The dull drumming of an engine brought them to their senses. Peering
through the swirling sea-mist the boys saw a large fishing boat looming.
They were directly in its path and it was on course to run them down.

But which way should they turn? One way would take them further and
further out to sea ... the other to the safety of shallower water and land.

Fighting back tears, the boys struggled to pull the boat round, just out of the
path of the fishing boat, but were still swamped by its powerful bow wave. Bailing
water with all his might, Angus hushed his brother. "Listen!", he called as he
strained to hear through the muffling sea-mist, "Listen!" He was sure he could
just make out the excited yelping of a dog, a dog who sounded very like Mick.

At the same time, there was a spluttering sound from a plane's engine, mysteriously flying low, skimming over the sea and visible now through the parting mists.

Hardly believing their eyes, the boys were amazed to see the outline of a World War I plane swooping over the water towards them. Leaning out of the cockpit, a leather-capped pilot and his dog gave them the thumbs up. Again, he passed low and close and waggled his wings for them to follow.

But follow him where? Into shallower waters and the safety of the shore?
Or further out, towards Harwich, the North Sea and Holland?

The mists began to swirl and thicken once again. Grabbing the
oars the boys began to pull madly on them, squinting to follow
the path of the plane, now rapidly disappearing ahead.

At last, the scraping of the boat on the gravely bottom of the shell beach
meant they had found their way back to the safety of the shore.

Almost instantly, the urgent barking of the dog, and the whirring of the
plane's engine stopped, and silence descended once more upon the beach.

Heaving to get their breath back, the boys hung limply over their oars, resting their aching muscles.

"Can you believe how lucky we've been?", exclaimed Hamish. "If the pilot of that World War I plane hadn't spotted us …" he shuddered.

Splashing and dragging the boat ashore, a puzzled frown spread across Angus's face. "That can't be right. The Red Arrows were flying first, then the Battle of Britain Flight. Isn't that a fly-past for World War II, not World War I?"

Their thoughts were interrupted as a lone figure strode down the beach towards them. Could this be the strange pilot who had guided them home to safety?

"Oh no", groaned the boys, as the familiar figure of their father loomed into focus. Dangling from his arms were the two forgotten lifejackets.

"He looks mad! Now we're for it!"

Hamish reddened and tried to explain to his father about the trip, the game with Mick, the sudden change in the weather, the pilot, the dog barking …

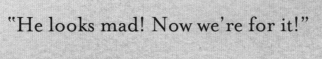

"How can I believe a story like that?" asked his father.

"The point is that you both forgot your life-jackets, you could both have drowned, and no really, I don't believe that you were rescued by some World War I pilot and his dog! I'm disappointed in you both, I want to trust you and let you take the boat out by yourselves, but now I'm not so sure."

His stinging words faded, as Angus, hoping to avoid most of his father's anger, rummaged around in his bag, playing with, and finally pulling out the parting gift dropped at his feet by his friend Mick.

It was a muddy jar. Peering into it he could just make out the shape of an envelope, together with a 1919 penny.

Pushing the jar into his father's hands, Angus waited for him to extract the yellowing envelope, and watched him carefully unfold it. He paused and drew a deep breath. Kneeling down in the sand, he showed the boys the handwritten note which read:

In memory of my dooted fox terrier
dog and friend "MICK" — Rest in peace
and may your spirit be in
Happy affectio... ever...
February 22nd 1927

But here the words became so fragile and faded that he could make out no more of the letters.

Turning it over,
the boys' father
pulled out a sheet
of notepaper, from
which he read:

Telegrams: Edgar Roberts East Mersea
Station: St. Botolphs, L & N.E.R.
Bankers: National and Provincial

IVY FARM
EAST MERSEA
ESSEX

THE MERSEA HERD OF
PEDIGREE LARGE BLACK PIGS
Reared on open air system
Bred from Best Strains

This is written hoping that it may never be disturbed - should it
be - to bear witness that on the 22nd day of February 1927
"Mick" the devoted Fox Terrier dog and long years' friend of
Edgar George Roberts of Ivy Farm passed away and was buried
here in the little wood belonging to the farm and called
Cudmore Grove.

Mick came as a puppy from Leicestershire to his master when
he was training as an air pilot at Northolt Aerodrome. He
flew with his Master and was always his companion except
when his Master went abroad to fight in the war. Mick was
an invincible fighter - a great ratter - a great sportsman
altogether and gentle and loving to all mankind.

Friends, if you have ever loved a dog, leave his earthly
remains in peace. I trust his spirit will have joined his
master in the other world.

Signed: Edgar George Robert

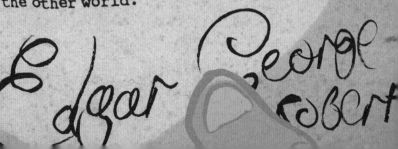

In the distance, a plane
spluttered, a dog barked ...

The End

The End Of A Doggy Tale?

How many islanders and visitors remember the little dog grave in
the bluebell wood at Cudmore Grove on Mersea Island?

I vividly remember Sunday walks and the excitement of racing along the cliff-path
with my brother and sisters to see who would reach Mick's gravestone first.

As the years passed, the walks continued, with the cliff-path gradually being eroded by the
sea. It moved closer and closer to the shore-edge, with much of it becoming impassable.
In the end it became too dangerous, and the path to Mick's grave was lost forever...

...That was until February 1988, when nine-year old Leon Butterfield from
Colchester was playing on the beach, and found an old jar at the tide's edge. It was
still sealed, and when opened contained a yellowing envelope and letter, together
with a photograph, totally without definition, but signed Edgar George Roberts,
Ivy Farm, East Mersea, February 22nd 1927. Also enclosed, was a 1919 penny,
perhaps to pay the ferryman to take Mick across the sea to the other world?

Many people may have wondered about Mick and his owner. And I did wonder who
was the dog's owner, and I wondered enough to find out, and I did wonder who
was the little boy who found the jar... and I wondered enough to find out...

But most of all, I wondered if I could mix up all these lovely elements, a dog's
grave, a World War I pilot and a young boy's beach find, into a second Mersea
Island Tale, beautifully illustrated by Tom, which I hope you've enjoyed.

Veronique

On England's most easterly inhabited island

Pilots, Pets and Planes

Second Lieutenant Edgar George Roberts

Clearly a man who not only loved his dog, but also served his country well.

Second Lieutenant Edgar George Roberts of Ivy Farm, whose heart was broken when he buried his doggy friend Mick in the little bluebell wood at Cudmore Grove on Mersea Island.

Pygmy Polish, 317 Squadron Mascot, RAF Northolt

During the First World War, pilots with their dogs were a common sight on the airfields, and there are many photographs of pilots with their four-legged aviator friends. Sadly, RAF Northolt could not provide photos of Edgar and Mick in the plane together – but they had this photo of Pygmy who belonged to Polish 317 squadron based at RAF Northolt – and I think he looks a bit like Mick!

Edgar Roberts represents the many hundreds of pilots who passed through the flying training courses at Northolt during the Great War (1914-18). Second Lieutenant Roberts (Number 3828) was commissioned into the RFC on 18 August 1916, following service as a Driver with the Honourable Artillery Company (HAC). He passed his Flying Certificate on 2 November 1916 (the Unit listed on his certificate refers to Military School, Ruislip). His early flying career involved training on Maurice Farman biplanes, before moving on to BE2cs. He was posted to No.205 Squadron of the Royal Air Force on 13 September 1918. This squadron had formerly been 'Naval 5' Squadron of the Royal Naval Air Service (RNAS) prior to the formation of the RAF on 1 April 1918. Whilst with No.205 Squadron, Roberts flew DH9s engaged upon bombing missions against the German Army during the Hundred Days Campaign.

Subsequently, he was attached to the Intelligence Corps at HQ 22 wing, which included temporary duty with No.211 Squadron (formerly 'Naval 11'), which also flew DH9s. Here Roberts was deployed on photographic reconnaissance and bombing operations against the German Army, which by this stage of the Great War was heavily engaged in a desperate fighting retreat prior to the Armistice on 11 November 1918.

With special thanks to Sgt Mark Bristow, En-Route Charts Editor (and Station Historian), AIDU, RAF Northolt.